HORSE DIARIES

· Koda ·

Horse's
Name

HORSE DIARIES

#1: Elska

#2: Bell's Star

#3: Koda

HORSE DIARIES

Koda

PATRICIA HERMES

illustrated by RUTH SANDERSON

RANDOM HOUSE 🏠 NEW YORK

Text copyright © 2009 by Patricia Hermes
Illustrations copyright © 2009 by Ruth Sanderson
Photo credits: © Filmfoto/Dreamstime.com (p. 137); Library of Congress (pp. 134–35); copyright © North Wind/North Wind Picture Archives (p. 132).

Published in the United States by Random House Children's Books,
a division of Random House, Inc., New York.

Random House and the colophon are registered trademarks of Random House, Inc.

Visit us on the Web! www.randomhouse.com/kids

Educators and librarians, for a variety of teaching tools, visit us at
www.randomhouse.com/teachers

Library of Congress Cataloging-in-Publication Data
Hermes, Patricia.
Koda / by Patricia Hermes ; illustrated by Ruth Sanderson. — 1st ed.
p.   cm. — (Horse diaries ; #3)
Summary: Traveling with his owners from Missouri to Oregon in 1848,
Koda, an energetic two-year-old quarter horse, finds the long journey
increasingly tedious and tiring until his young owner goes missing
on the trail and he must use all his skills to find her.
ISBN 978-0-375-85199-5 (trade) — ISBN 978-0-375-95199-2 (lib. bdg.)
1. Quarter horse—Juvenile fiction. 2. Oregon National Historic Trail—
Juvenile fiction. [1. Quarter horse—Fiction. 2. Horses—Fiction.
3. Oregon National Historic Trail—Fiction. 4. Overland journeys to the Pacific—
Fiction. 5. West (U.S.)—History—To 1848—Fiction.]
I. Sanderson, Ruth, ill. II. Title.
PZ10.3.H466Ko 2009   [Fic]—dc22   2008034836

Printed in the United States of America

10 9 8

First Edition

CONTENTS

"Oh! if people knew what a comfort to horses a light hand is . . ."
—from *Black Beauty*, by Anna Sewell

HORSE DIARIES
· Koda ·

Independence, Missouri,
Early Spring, 1846

On that quiet spring morning, there was nothing but green grass and sun and the smell of my mama. I nuzzled her and she moved closer so I could have more of her warm, sweet milk. There was so much I didn't

know yet, so much she promised to show me.
But I had already found out scores of things
on my own. I was just three days old, but I
bet I knew more than lots of older horses. I
knew that the small white furballs on the
hillside that Mama called sheep didn't care
at all about playing. They didn't care even if
I pranced up to them and said, *Come on, let's
play.* And they sure didn't want to race.
There were other things on that hillside that
looked kind of like sheep. But they didn't
move at all, and that's how I learned they
were rocks.

*Rocks just sit in one place all day long, year
after year,* my mama said, *just soaking up sun
and snow, which comes later.*

Rocks didn't move even when I nudged

one with my nose. I was awful glad that I wasn't born a rock.

My mama told me, and then told me again, that I was much too curious. She said I had to watch out and not get too bold. But she was gentle when she said these things. I knew she liked my spirit, and I told her that I liked my spirit, too. My mama whinnied when I said that. Then she told me to lie down and rest because we had a long day before us. We were heading back to the herd, she said. She'd gone off alone for a time, away from the herd, once she knew that I was about to be born. She wanted me all to herself for a while, and I understood that. Like I told my mama, I was learning a whole lot of things already.

Still, why rest when the sun was up and shining, and the wind was blowing like anything? So just for fun, I went zooming around the hillside, my mane flying in the wind. I felt the sun, warm on my back. My legs had been all wobbly for the first day or so, but not now. Now they felt like they were attached to me real good. They moved me along so fast I was even leaping around at times. And then I saw something new.

It was small, sort of round, with prickly things on it. And it wasn't moving. Well, how could anything not move on a day like this?

I nosed up to it.

No, it wasn't a rock. Then why hold so still? It had pointing kinds of things sticking out all over its body. It seemed to be looking

at me. Even now, young as I was, I knew that rocks didn't look at you. I placed my nose down close.

And then, like the wind itself had roared up to my side, suddenly my mama was there. Her body seemed to swell, filling the air beside me. I could feel the heat of her nearness. Her eyes were wild, her ears laid back.

Foolish colt! she said. *Come away! Now.*

She shoved her shoulder into me, almost making me fall to the ground. I backed away.

Follow me. Come! she said.

And she turned tail, flying back up the hillside toward the trees where we had been. I liked this race, and I ran on ahead. But my mama caught up and passed me. She stopped short, so short that I couldn't stop. I bumped her big side. Then I tumbled back a bit. I stumbled over a rock, and then I was lying on the ground. I looked up at her, surprised. I got my long legs back under me and untangled myself and stood up. But one leg ached. When I looked down, I saw a thin stream of blood running down my flank.

Was this some kind of game? I didn't like it.

No, it wasn't a game. I had not seen my mama like this before, but I knew what it was. She was very angry.

She lowered her head and looked in my eyes. *That was a porcupine. It could prick those quills right into your face. They would hurt worse than that fall you just took.*

Oh.

My pride was wounded, so I looked away. *It doesn't hurt much,* I said.

Never mind hurt! my mama said, still angry-like. *Those quills get in your face and you would swell all up. You wouldn't be able to eat. To nurse. You'd starve to death.*

Well, I had learned enough by now to know that I had just been born, and I sure liked it here. And I knew that death wouldn't be what I'd want for a real long time.

I hung my head, ashamed-like. I guess I did have a lot to learn.

Curious is good, my mama said, and now she sounded not as angry. *Foolish is not!*

Yes, Mama.

She seemed to relent some, because she whinnied at me, telling me to look up. I did, and looked high in the sky. There were birds flying all about, wild black ones, and one that soared and swooped low. Mama said the soaring one was an eagle. I wondered what it would be like to be born an eagle, to have wings instead of legs and hooves. Then we saw an ugly-faced one that kept swooping down to look at something on the hillside.

My mama got quiet when that big bird flew by, and she didn't say anything about it, but I could tell that she didn't like it much. I nudged myself closer, and Mama nudged me back.

What, Mama? I asked her.

A buzzard, my mama answered. *They're mean old birds. Come only when something is dead or dying.*

And then, because my mama was a little quiet, and I knew I had frightened her with that porcupine, and maybe she was thinking that buzzard would come for me if I was dead, well, I decided maybe she needed me to rest right close by her side for a while.

I closed my eyes and lay down, my legs stretched out. The sun was warm, and so many things whirled around inside my head. My mama was nearby. She liked my spirit. And soon we would go back and meet the herd. Mama said most of the herd horses were like us, quarter horses. That meant we could run very, very fast, the fastest quarter mile that any horse on earth could run. Well, I knew that. I knew I was the fastest horse already. I flicked my ears a little bit when I was half-asleep, just to let Mama know I was still there with her, maybe dreaming some. And then she was nudging me.

Time to get up, my little colt.

Well, she didn't have to tell me twice.

I was up and ready to go, wanting so

much to go back to those other horses Mama
had told me about. She told me then what
the others would call me. I had been given a
name already. Koda, it was. She said that it
had a special meaning, but she wouldn't tell
me what it was. She said I would find out,
but not yet.

Of course that set me to wondering, but

everything set me to wondering. Still, wondering didn't stop me from moving. And moving was all I wanted to do.

We started off then, the two of us, ranging over that hillside, my mama in the lead, seeming to know just where she was going, straight and true. I kept running on ahead, and my mama kept whinnying me back to her. Always I came back, because she sure knew where she was going, and I sure did not. But with the sun high and that wind blowing right by me, ruffling my mane and tickling at my nose, it was mighty hard to hold back.

You'll tire yourself out, my little colt, my mama said more than one time. *You're wasting that fine energy.*

But it took more energy to hold back, so at times I went zooming past Mama, my tail flying right out behind me. Once, I scared myself some, because I couldn't see her any longer. But then I heard her whinnying, and I came back. I was so happy thinking about what awaited us, wondering what the other horses would be like. I knew that we would also be meeting creatures Mama called humans. She said there was one small human who was waiting for me, the girl who had given me my name.

Why did she name me, Mama? I asked. *Why didn't you give me my name?*

You'll see, Mama answered. *You'll learn about humans.*

She sounded a bit worried-like when she said "humans," but she wouldn't tell me more about them. She said we needn't be worrying over them for a while yet. But I thought she did seem happy when she told me about the small human who had named me.

Well, if my mama wasn't worrying, then I wasn't, either. We ran a long way, over meadows, over the hillside, the wind swooping by every now and then, like its job was just for us, to cool us off. After a while, though, it was really hot—even with the wind helping us out—and Mama found some shade under a tree. She ate some of the young spring grass, and then she spent a long time drinking from a stream nearby. I had no interest in that water stuff. I had her milk, all that I wanted.

We rested awhile then, and I have to say, I needed that rest. The day was hot and I had been running hard. But just when I was ready to say it was time for some sleep, what did my mama do? She upped and started meandering away.

I didn't budge. Not me. Time for sleep.

My mama kept going, and never even looked back to see me. So I knew there was nothing to do but follow. I was mighty slow, though, barely able to keep my head high. But then my curiosity came back, and before I knew it, I was in the lead. Maybe just that little bit of rest did it, or maybe my mama's milk, but all the energy I'd had that morning came rushing back. I took off over flats and up hills. I found, too, that I could see lots more than I had been able to see just the day before. I bet I could see now almost as good as my mama could see. I knew I could see better than I saw that first day, right after I was born. And now, way off in the distance, I saw something interesting. It moved, so I knew it wasn't a rock.

It was also way too big to be a porcupine. It just sat atop a boulder real quiet-like, seeming almost the same color as the rock, just its tail moving a bit at the tip. A stump? I had scared a bunch of stumps this morning. Maybe this would be another fine stump to get after. But I had already figured out that stumps didn't move and they didn't have tails, though sometimes from a distance they looked like they did. So this was something new, something to nose out and see what it was up to.

This time when I came near, I was a bit more cautious. I had learned something from that porcupine, and I wasn't about to be tricked again. So I ambled up close, but not so close that my nose could get pricked.

I was still a good distance away, but even so, I could tell that this thing did not smell

nice. Also, my instincts were maybe working
better than they had this morning and were
telling me to beware. I pranced backward,
looking over my shoulder for my mama.

Mama! Where was my mama?

And then, when my head was turned, this thing that was not a stump or a porcupine, this thing leaped off the top of that rock. It came at me. It was all fur and twitching ears and claws that stretched out toward me. And it had a foul smell.

I leaped backward.

Mama!

There was no Mama! There was no time to wait. And this was no time to play. This creature didn't like horses, or maybe liked us too well, maybe for dinner, and I had a feeling I would be dead if it caught up with me. So I lit out. I had new, strong legs to carry me, and they carried me away like the wind.

I leaped over the range, my heart thundering in time to the beat of my legs pounding the ground. I leaped over streams, then scrambled up a knoll, scattering rocks. I was slipping and sliding, but I went on. I darted side to side, knowing somehow that was better than a straight line. After a long while, a long, long while, my heaving sides were begging me to stop, and I did. I looked behind me. I listened. I sniffed the air.

My breath came all raggedy, and my heart was beating and thundering in my chest. No creature with claws and twitching ears and tail was chasing me. Nothing.

Mama. I needed to tell my mama. I was safe. And I had learned something else. I had learned from the porcupine. I'd learned to be smart. I didn't know what that creature was, but it was gone. And I was still here.

I looked around. *Mama.* Where was my mama?

Mama?

Only the wind answered me. Mama was nowhere to be seen.

Going Home

Then I was even more scared than I had been by that wild thing. Where was my mama? I needed her. I knew so many things already, and that was one thing I knew, that I needed a mama. I was thirsty, too, aching for some of her milk.

Mama? I called again. I held still, listening. *Mama?*

Nothing answered me, nothing but the wind moving through the trees. Darkness was setting in, too, the sun sliding behind those rocks that didn't move. Everything turned pink, and then a little purple, and I got to say, it was mighty pretty. I even stood there awhile, just breathing it all in, before the fear came back again.

Where was my mama? Where was that herd of horses she'd told me about? I didn't know how to find my way home. I didn't even know where home was. Why did Mama leave me this way?

And then I realized—she hadn't left me. I'd left her. That nasty-smelling thing had scared me and I ran. She wouldn't leave me. I knew that all right.

So my job was to find her. But first, rest. My legs were good and strong. I wasn't wobbly anymore. But I surely was worn-out. I'd rest, just a little bit.

I lay down, my long legs stretched out, aching for some milk, my stomach so empty. But even hungry as I was, sleep came over me, and when I slept, I dreamed. I dreamed of my mama, that she was nosing against my side, pushing herself against me, whispering, *There, there, little colt, all is well. Rest. In the morning, we'll return to the herd.*

But, Mama, I told her in my sleep, *I don't know where the herd is.*

And then she nudged me real hard, and

it wasn't a dream mama but a real live one, my mama, my very own!

I scrambled to my feet, as unsteady as if I'd just been born, and I pushed my nose into her side and drank her milk, and drank and drank. I didn't say a thing till I'd had my fill.

I lifted my head and Mama nudged me, playful-like. *Foolish colt,* she said. She didn't sound angry, though. She sounded somewhat proud. *Foolish colt to get so close.*

I didn't get close, Mama! I said. *I learned from that porcupine. And I was tricky, too. I ran zigzag, not in a straight line. Wasn't I smart, Mama?*

Mama didn't answer that. She just said, *You learned how fast a cougar can run.*

He smelled horrid, Mama, I said.

You learned that, too, my mama said. *To trust your nose. If it smells bad, stay away. Cougars and coyotes and wolves and bears, they all smell nasty. Now, let's rest a bit. As soon as it's light, we'll be on our way.*

Well, that suited me just fine. But I

had to know one last thing before I slept. *Where were you, Mama? When that cougar was chasing me, where were you? Why didn't you whinny me back to you?*

Mama nudged me close. *I led him away from you, little wild colt,* she said. *I ran slow. I even limped some. He wanted you, a soft, newborn colt. But he didn't know how fast a quarter horse can run. He saw me lame and thought I'd be easy to catch. I wasn't.*

Oh, Mama, I said. *I'm so glad he didn't catch you. Or me!*

And for the second time that day, I felt ashamed of myself. I thought I knew so much. I had so much to learn.

Darkness settled around us then, and a nighttime sun came up—Mama called it *moon.* Moon climbed high over the treetops and glimmered down on us, and it was so pretty that I thought I'd watch it awhile. But I guess I was just too tuckered out, because I slept. And next thing I knew, moon was gone, the sun was up warming the treetops, and Mama and I had breakfasted and were on our way. My legs felt stronger even than the day before. And so I started out running fast and hard, my mane whipping in the wind. But that whole morning, I never got so far away that I couldn't see my mama. I had learned my lesson!

We loped along fine and steady till the sun was high and hot, and then we rested in the shade of some cottonwoods. It felt mighty good, but after I was rested, I meandered out into the sun, and I found something new to interest me. It was a long brown speckled thing, coiled up atop a rock. It had eyes, so I could tell it was a live creature, but I had learned a lot about creatures already, so I didn't nose it out or get too close. I just pranced around it a little bit, wondering if it wanted to play.

A snake, my mama said, seeing me prancing around like that. *Don't get close. Snakes are like cougars. Not your friends, my little colt.*

Well, the snake had not much of a smell, and he didn't seem too friendly anyway, so I backed off to let him sleep in the sun, if that's what he wanted.

And then Mama began wandering off again. We traveled a long way after that, a really long way, not stopping at all but for Mama to drink at a stream, and for me to nurse awhile.

All day we loped, till the sun was low in the sky. I didn't want to say it to Mama, but I was tired. I didn't think I could go on any-more. But just when my legs were about to buckle, Mama stopped atop a small hill. Beside us, a wild river rushed along, bubbling and gurgling. A soft mist rose off it, and grass grew lush and green all around.

Before us was a wide open plain, and beyond that, another sloping hillside, and strung out on that plain—well, what I saw, I'll just never forget. My first sight of the herd, horses just like Mama and me. So many of them! But when I looked closer, I saw that

they weren't exactly like us. Some were bigger, and some of them smaller. *Colts!* I said.

Fillies, *too*, Mama said.

Then one of those big horses whinnied up at us, and Mama whinnied back. I didn't know what they were saying to one another, but I couldn't help myself, and I decided to chime right in. I raised up my head and did my own whinnying, my first ever. It seemed to me I'd done it right fine, if I do say so myself.

And then the one who had whinnied at us, a huge red-brown stallion, came jogging up the hill to us, his eyes shining, his fine head tossing, his ears pricked forward.

That's Lika, my mama said. *Your sire.*

Sire? My father?

Lika was a majestic horse, far, far bigger than Mama, and he came to a stop right in front of us. I tell you true, I was kind of scared, and I could feel my heart galloping hard inside me. I leaned against Mama's side, never taking my eyes off him.

He rubbed nostrils with Mama, and she rubbed his back and didn't move away, and I figured the two of them were saying howdy. And then that big stallion started in circling us, like he was looking me over, his big head right close to my flank. At that, Mama whirled about at him, and her ears went back, and she bared her teeth. But she didn't nip at him, just kept her eyes on him, like she was saying, *You watch yourself,* and I knew that she was making sure he knew who was who when it came to protecting me. But it seemed then that I didn't need protecting, not from him, anyway, because after a minute, he pushed his nostrils gently against mine, and I smelled him good and he smelled me back. I liked what I smelled and

didn't feel so scared anymore. He nosed up to
Mama again, then turned away and trotted
down the hillside and back to the herd.

I watched him go, his big, wide reddish
flanks, his black mane and tail flowing, his
coat shining with little circles as the setting
sun glinted off it. And then, as he returned to

the herd, I saw something odd and couldn't figure it out.

Another horse. A horse with something on its back. Galloping toward us.

Mama? I asked. I quick sidestepped till I was behind her, almost tangling myself in my own legs in my hurry. Mama didn't seem scared, though, and raised her head and nickered, welcoming this new creature.

A *human*, she told me. *Jasmine, the human who named you.*

And then this human was beside us, and—oh my. She and the horse were not just one. She slid down, separating herself from the horse. And there stood that horse, and it looked just like me and Mama, though it still had something on its back.

A *saddle*, Mama said, seeing my look.

Then Jasmine began making squeaking, squealing noises, and I tell you, it hurt my ears, but Mama didn't seem to mind at all. Jasmine threw herself at Mama, draped herself over Mama's neck, and Mama nosed her up and down, welcoming her!

"Rosie! Rosie, you're back!" Jasmine cried. "With your beautiful foal! With Koda. Oh, I can't wait to tell Papa!"

Then Jasmine threw herself at me, and I thought Mama would bare her teeth at her, but no, Mama let her touch me. I quivered. My flesh almost hurt at her touch. But just for a moment. Because she was burying her face in my coat and making happy sounds, rubbing my belly and my flank. I knew then,

from her sounds and her touch and her smell,
that she was safe to be with.

Jasmine kept on leaning her head against
me, all the while rubbing my coat and patting

my face. "Beautiful! Just beautiful!" she said to me. "Do you know that? You're beautiful. My dear Koda, my new friend! And that's what your name means, did you know that?"

Well, I didn't know, but I made a whinnying sound at her because I had just learned how to whinny. Besides, I liked her immediately.

She laughed, so I knew that she knew that I liked her. "Yes. It means 'friend'!" she said. "*Koda* is a Sioux Indian word for 'friend.' We will be friends forever, you and me, pretty Koda!"

I turned my head to Mama then. Was that all right—to be friends with Jasmine? I already liked her very much. But I belonged to Mama, didn't I? Mama was just nibbling at the grass and didn't seem concerned, so I guessed it was all right. In fact, it made me very, very happy to have a new friend, though I can't say I understood everything that I was feeling.

But there was one feeling I did understand—how tired I was. The sun was almost down, and I was hungry and I so much wanted to meet the herd. I moved gently away from Jasmine and over to my mama. Mama moved closer to me, allowing me to nurse, and she pushed her head against Jasmine, telling her to leave us alone.

Right away, Jasmine understood, and she moved toward her horse and leaped up. "Good night!" she said. "I'll be back tomorrow. And as soon as I can, I'll bring my papa to meet you."

When Jasmine was gone, I wanted to ask Mama more about her, and even about her papa. And I wanted to meet the herd. But I was so tired. So all I said was, *Mama? Can we rest awhile?*

Yes, my mama said. *We'll sleep now. We'll meet the herd tomorrow. We're both tired. I'll need much energy and strength for the meeting.*

Why, Mama? I asked.

You'll see, Mama said.

Well, that was all right with me. Because by then, the stars were beginning to come out, and moon came with them, and below us, the horses all became quiet and still for the night. When I was finished nursing, I lay down at my mama's feet, feeling warm and happy. Tomorrow we would meet the herd.

Meeting the Herd

The sun was just creeping above the trees when I scrambled to my feet. Mama had moved off a ways into a soft glen and was nibbling at that bright green grass. Below us, I could hear the herd awakening, feel the rumbling and muttering of hooves. I wondered why they hadn't moved up the hillside to us, the way my sire had done. But then I figured they were just waiting to see what would happen with my mama. I remembered the way she had bared her teeth at my sire, and maybe the others were scared she'd nip at them, too. I already knew how fierce and brave Mama was.

I moved up beside her and began to nurse. After a while, I asked, *Now, Mama? Can we go down now, Mama?*

Come, she said. *Stay close.*

We trotted through the meadows and grasses, the river running alongside us, Mama leading the way, me tight behind her, feeling excited and a little scared all at once. It took a while to reach the herd, because it seemed they had moved on in the night. Or maybe it was that my eyesight had gotten better, and things weren't quite what they had seemed the day before.

Anyway, soon we were close. And closer. And I tell you, my heart was racing almost as bad as when the twitchy-eared critter took off after me. But the smell was all right. These horses smelled fine, the way horses should smell, and I began to calm down.

At the bottom of the hill, Mama stopped. Then, slowly, she moseyed right into that crowd of horses, and right away, they came nosing in to see.

I stayed behind my mama. A big stallion, a bay just like me, came up to us, and Mama whirled around at him. He moved back, but he didn't seem to mean me harm. He just circled us lazily. And then another bay came up, and another, and then a little pinto pony, and then some colts—my size! Mama told me what each one was named, but there were so many, I couldn't remember. I remembered only two—one of the colts and the pinto pony—and that's just because they were kind of like me. The colt was called Will and the pinto was Gilgo. Seeing that they were about my size, I thought maybe they'd want to play. I began to ease away from Mama's side, not too far, just a little, and I kept an eye on her.

Mama was busy making it plain to the other horses who was the boss of me. She kept shoving and nudging at the ones who came up to inspect me, and a few times, she took a little nip at the sides of the bigger ones who got too pushy. But it was pretty clear, even to me, that none of them meant me any harm. They were just curious, that's all.

After they had all nosed around me, they seemed to tire of me, all but Will and Gilgo.

Come run! Will said.

Well, running was what I did best. But did I dare leave my mama?

Mama was trading talk with some mares, and it seemed to me that the mares were kind of excited, switching their ears back and forth, maybe talking proud about their new colts and fillies—Mama, too. I moved a little further from Mama then, still not quite sure if I should, till she said, Go on, *little colt. Go run.*

Well, that was about all I needed to hear.

So I took off, with Will right on my heels and that little pinto, Gilgo, trailing not far behind. The sun was high by then, and the wind at my back, and I ran, head up, sniffing the air.

Will raced past me, then whirled around and began to leap, bucking his rear legs up, his back bent, then straightening out and doing it all over again.

I just watched him. It looked fun, so I asked him, *What is that? How do you do that?*

Crow-hopping, he said, and he showed me how it was done. It took me a few tries, but before I knew it, I could crow-hop just like him, like I'd been doing it my whole life. And the two of us went bounding about—sometimes racing, sometimes crow-hopping—

all over the place. Gilgo tried to crow-hop, too, but I think she wasn't as young as we were, and she didn't do so well.

We went on playing most of that morning, racing one another, and it was clear that we were good runners. Running is what quarter horses do best, my mama had told me, and it was sure fun to test it all out. I won most of the races.

By noon, with the sun so hot, I was just about worn-out, so I went and found my mama and had me a good drink till I was filled up. I lay down then, in the shade of the cottonwoods alongside the river, and I must have slept. Because next thing I knew, there was the sound of hooves, moving fast, and I scrambled to my feet. Something new to see.

Coming up alongside the river were two horses with riders on their backs.

Well, I went and found my mama and asked what was happening.

Maybe herding us back to the homestead and our human family, my mama said. *Some of the herd roam free in summertime. Some of us don't. You'll see.*

And though I didn't know what a family or a homestead was, or why we were going there, Mama had raised her head and was nickering at the coming riders, so I knew that it wasn't something to be worried about.

Soon those riders were upon us, and then I nickered, too—for one of them was Jasmine. She rode up right beside me and then leaped off her horse, throwing her arms around me and nuzzling herself against me, just like she had the day before.

I rubbed my head up and down, up and down against her while she patted me, letting her know how much I liked her touch.

"Oh, Koda!" she said. "Good morning, my beautiful colt!"

She turned then to a male human who had just dismounted. That one was rubbing my mama's head and ears, and Mama was welcoming him with little nickering sounds. *This is Jasmine's papa,* Mama said to me.

"Papa!" Jasmine cried. "Come look! Come meet Koda!"

Mama whinnied again and moved closer to me, and I could see that she was proud to show me off. Jasmine's papa came and looked

me over real good, running his hands over
my flanks, my back and chest and belly, and
Mama didn't seem at all worried about that.
He stroked my mane and tugged gently at my
ears and whispered to me. I could tell from

his voice and his touch that he was a good human.

When he was all finished exploring me, he turned to Jasmine and put his arm around her. "Jasmine," he said, "I believe Rosie's produced the best colt ever!"

Jasmine leaned into her papa, just the way I lean into my mama sometimes. "He's beautiful, isn't he?" she said. "Papa? Mama will love him, won't she? I can't wait for her to see him. I bet he'll make Mama feel better."

"He will," her papa said. "We'll trot Koda right up close to her veranda this afternoon."

"And when Mama's better," Jasmine said, "and when Koda's older, all three of us can ride together."

"We'll do just that, sweetheart," he said.

"Now, come on, let's get these two down home. I've got work to do."

He turned back to my mama, and Jasmine put her head against mine. "Wait till you meet my mama!" she whispered. "She'll love you. But she's sick, Koda. She coughs all the time. But don't worry, the minute she sees you, she'll feel better."

Well, I wasn't worrying, except then Jasmine held out her hand, and over her arm was—could it be? It was—a snake!

I reared back, but Jasmine only laughed. "It's a rope," she said. "It's just a lead rope. Want to smell it?"

She held it out to me. I backed off some more. Snakes are like cougars, Mama had said. They're not our friends.

"It's just a lead rope!" Jasmine said again. "Here, sniff it up good. I promise it won't hurt you."

Well, I had already learned about what to trust and what to not—what was good and what was bad. And Jasmine was good. So I leaned my head in—but not too close— and sniffed at that rope.

It didn't smell bad, but it didn't smell good, either. It was just plain.

Jasmine's horse had bent his head and was nibbling at some grass, and he didn't seem afraid, so I figured it was all right to sniff some more.

"See?" Jasmine said when I'd had my fill. "Now, try this." She looped a rope and slid it gently over my nose and ears. "This is a halter. Does it feel all right? Can you stand it? It won't hurt you."

Then she fastened a long rope to the halter. It didn't hurt. But it felt bad, and I looked at my mama.

It's all right, Mama said. *It's a halter and lead rope. They won't hurt you.*

She was standing docile and quiet as Jasmine's papa put a halter and lead rope on her. Well, if it was fine with her, it was all right with me, too, though I can't say I liked it much.

And then Jasmine got atop her horse, and she urged me to run beside her, so of course I did, though I tossed my head this way and that, with the strange feel of that rope tugging at me. Still, it wasn't a bad feeling once I got used to it. Then, once my mama came up alongside, and Jasmine's papa came alongside atop his horse, we all went galloping down the hill to that homestead my mama had told me about.

When we finally halted, Jasmine got off her horse and tethered him to a tree. Then she began walking slowly, leading me by the rope, away from my mama, gentle-like, talking to me the whole time and showing me things.

The first thing she showed me was the place where she lived—her house, she called it—and she said that they slept and ate inside of this place. To me, it looked like a row of tree trunks without leaves, laid sideways, with a roof on top, and I wondered why she'd want to sleep in there and not out under the stars.

And then she showed me a barn and creatures
called cows and another creature called a dog.
She picked up the dog so that I could see him

good. His name was Honey and she said he was her favorite dog in the whole world, but I can tell you, he was a mighty little creature, no bigger than the baby rabbits I'd seen bounding around the meadows.

There were also humans everywhere. Some were big, and one was small, kind of like Jasmine, except smaller. Her name was Violet and she was Jasmine's baby sister. And then I got to meet Jasmine's mama, but we didn't stop to visit long, because her mama was feeling poorly. I could tell that from the way she coughed and coughed, and how she had to rest herself against Jasmine. But she was awfully pretty, and she said she thought I was the mightiest colt ever.

There were so many other things to see

and sniff out and learn about, but then I began bucking back against that rope again, tossing my head, because suddenly I was hungry and thirsty.

"Oh, Koda!" Jasmine cried. "I'm sorry! You need your mama, don't you?"

I did. And I was so glad that she knew what I felt the moment I felt it.

She turned right around and led me back the way we'd come. I pricked up my ears and walked smartly then, looking this way and that, so happy at all that I was seeing in my new homestead. I felt kind of proud of all that I knew, and I couldn't wait to tell my mama all about it.

I figured my mama would be as proud of me as I was of myself.

Two Thousand Miles to Go

For the next two years, I roamed the pastures with other horses—older ones and some colts and fillies, too—once I had been branded and marked. I wasn't old enough to be ridden yet, so Jasmine often rode up alongside me on her horse, talking to me and teaching me things. At first, I didn't go far—never out of sight of my mama and the corral—because I was still nursing and I liked knowing that my mama was nearby. But after a while, I didn't need my mama's milk so much and began nibbling at the grasses, and I wandered further and further.

When winter came on, we were all herded back to the corral. The snows fell and everything was frozen and still, and I could paw hard at the ground and find not even one little shoot of green grass. When that happened, Jasmine and her papa made sure that Mama and I and all the horses had plenty of hay to eat and a good portion of oats once in a while.

And so for those two years, I lived that way—roaming the pastures in summer, and holed up in the corral and the barn in winter. That second winter, Jasmine came into the barn one morning and wept into my side, hugging me close. Her mama had died in the night, and her baby sister, too, and after that, for days and weeks on end, she didn't visit me very much. And when she did, she and her papa both, their heads were bowed low, as though they were carrying a mighty weight on themselves. Jasmine seemed to be sickly, too, and she coughed the way her mama had coughed that day I first met her.

And then, the year I turned two, in the early part of the springtime, when the soft winds had just begun to blow, Jasmine came running to the barn one morning. She had begun visiting the barn again every morning, and it seemed that some of her happy spirits had come back. Each day she whispered stories to me about a place called Oregon. Now, on this morning, she threw herself at me, hugging my neck hard, just the way she used to do.

"We're going, Koda!" Jasmine cried. "We're going to Oregon! We're going on the Oregon Trail! We're going to gallop along for miles and miles and miles. Papa says the air is clear in Oregon, and I'll stop coughing, and we'll build a whole new life there. So Papa sold everything, well, almost everything, and he bought some oxen and a big wagon and put all of our things in it that we want to bring along. And we're going to join the wagon train by the river! It's just a mile

or so from here, and our wagon and oxen are already there all loaded up and ready! And guess what, Koda? You're coming with us, and your mama, too. Aren't you happy?"

She gave me another one of her fierce

hugs, then raced from the barn, almost trip-
ping over her little dog, Honey. She stopped
and picked him up, then twirled around with
him in her arms, as if she was dancing.

Well. Imagine galloping free with Jasmine for days and days and miles and miles!
Later that morning, when we were set out to
pasture, I told Mama about all that Jasmine
had said and how happy I was. Mama already
knew about it. She said that all the mares
had been talking. Then Mama said she'd
been on other trail rides, and they were
sometimes hard.

Well, I didn't care if it was hard. Miles
and miles of running free! So then I offered
to race with Mama. She acted real impatient
with me then and told me that I had gotten

a big head even thinking that I could beat her in a race.

You're still a youngster, Mama said. *You have a lot to learn.* She even pretended to nip me some—though I knew she'd never hurt me.

Well, then I'd just have to race the wind. And I did—I lit out across the pasture, the wind whipping up my tail and mane. Some of the colts came chasing me, and all of us ran hard.

For the next few days, things went on this way—spring coming on, the wind freshening, the grass just beginning to green up. And then one morning, Jasmine and her papa arrived to lead us down to the river.

When Jasmine put that halter and lead rope on me, I couldn't stop prancing and tossing around, I was so happy. Jasmine was atop another horse, and I trotted alongside. Jasmine's papa was astride my mama. All of us then went jogging along the riverbank to the place where the wagons were gathered.

When we got there, Jasmine dismounted and tied her horse to a wagon. And then, just as she had when I had first come to the homestead, she began showing me things, pointing them out and explaining. The first things she showed me were some huge beasts, much, much bigger than horses, with large, curved horns. They were as wide as the widest tree trunks I had yet seen and looked to be sturdy like rocks or boulders. I didn't get close enough to smell them good, but they seemed gentle enough.

"Those are oxen, Koda," Jasmine said. "They'll pull our wagons. There are two or even four of them for each wagon. Sometimes horses pull wagons, too, and then the wagons can go faster. But Papa says that's too hard on the horse. And there are the wagons. See? All stretched out in the line? There are almost a hundred wagons, Papa says!"

I looked all about me. As far as I could see were those covered wagons, one after the other in a long line. They were tall and high off the ground, like fat white clouds that had dropped out of the sky.

"All these wagons are going with us," Jasmine said. "Papa says it will take six whole months. Two thousand miles, Koda! Papa showed it all to me on a map last night. Oh, Koda, I'm so excited. I've never seen or done anything big in my whole life, and now, I'm going to see the whole country! With you! And when we get there, you'll be old enough for me to ride!"

She fingered a string of pink beads around her neck then. "This is my mama's," she said. "I wear it always. I wish she was going with us."

That made me sad. I had liked her mama. I sure wouldn't want my mama to die.

Jasmine stroked my head as we walked on. "Now, this is our wagon," she said. "It's like a little house, all fixed up inside. We have supplies—flour and coffee and bacon

and lots and lots of grain for you and your
mama, because there may not be enough
grass to eat along the trail. We have a table
and a chair and bedding. We even have a

bed for Honey! And the wagon next to us is
for my aunt Agatha and uncle Henry and my
cousins. My cousin Sam will take turns with

Papa driving our wagon, so that Papa can ride with the scouts sometimes. Sam is sixteen, almost a man. They're even taking a milk cow along!"

She led me around the side of the wagon. "And now, see that?" she said, pointing. "That's a water barrel. And that's a cabinet for cooking pans and medicine. And you're going to walk right along behind our wagon until you're big enough for me to ride. And I'll walk with you. Jed says it's easier to walk than ride in the wagon because of how bumpy it is. And when we get to Oregon, Papa says you'll be a great help clearing the land and you can even take me to school!"

Jasmine stopped and leaned against me. "Oh, Koda, I'm just running on as though you understand about Mama and school and Oregon and clearing land, but I think you do. Don't you?"

She stroked my neck, and I rubbed my head up and down against her, letting her know that I did understand. At least, I understood some. What I understood was that the humans all around me were real busy. They were scurrying about the wagons, carrying all sorts of odd things that I had never seen before. Some male humans were on horses. The horses seemed well cared for, and they nickered at me, welcoming me, because horses are herd animals and we like to be together.

"Those men on horseback, Koda?" Jasmine said. "They're scouts. They'll ride ahead and look out for danger. The scouts will also look for places to stop and rest. And see what the men are carrying? Those are guns. They're for keeping away the wolves and cougars and bad things."

Those were scary words—*wolves* and *cougars*. I was older now and knew more about wolves and cougars and knew well how dangerous they were to horses. I shook my head, tossing it against the lead rope.

"Don't worry, Koda," Jasmine said. "That's why the men have guns. To protect us. They may even be able to shoot wild game for us to eat. And they'll look for places to water the oxen and horses, too. This is going to be a real adventure!"

Well, after having been cooped up in the corral and the barn all winter, I was real happy to be going on an adventure. Except just then I saw something that I didn't much like.

A human. A man. He was up on a horse, and the way he rode that horse, I knew right away the man was a bad one. His horse was all lathered up and had been ridden hard, and his sides were heaving and froth was

coming out of his mouth. The man rode up in front of Jasmine and me and stopped the horse with a mean pull of the reins, jerking the horse's head sideways.

"That colt coming with us?" the man asked. "How old is he?"

"Two," Jasmine said, and I could feel the fear—or was it anger?—coming from her. "This is Koda. He's Rosie's colt."

"Is he broke to saddle? Can you ride him?" the man asked.

"Not yet," Jasmine said, and she moved closer to me and wrapped an arm around my neck. "Koda," she said to me, "this is Jed. He's the elected leader of the wagon train. He's been on the trail before and knows the way."

"And I know other things, too," Jed said.

"I know what happens to horses on the trail, and it ain't pretty. Not enough grass. They get picky about the water. They get sick. You think you can carry enough grain for him?" Jed moved his horse closer to me, so close that I could feel the sweat coming off of his horse. "What good is a horse that can't be worked or ridden? Leave him behind. He's not big and strong enough yet. If he gets sick and weak on the trail, he won't last two hundred miles. He'll get eaten by wolves or coyotes."

I shuddered, and Jed's horse, who had been ridden so hard, shook his head, spraying foam from his mouth all around. He inched himself and his rider closer to me. *Pay Jed no mind,* he said. *I been on the trail before. You're young. You'll do fine. Just keep your wits about you, that's all. And keep on the lookout for wolves.*

Jed had just started to yank him around when Jasmine's papa came riding up on top of my mama. He reined to a stop in front of us and turned to Jed. "Are you trying to scare my daughter?" he asked. He smiled at Jed, but his voice sounded stern.

"Just telling her the truth, Mark," Jed said. "Can't believe how dumb you're being. Why do you want to bring along a horse that's no use to you? Sell the colt. He'll bring good money. It's going to be hard enough for that mare you're sitting atop of."

"Jed, we been all over this," Jasmine's papa said. "I've sold the rest of my herd. Koda belongs to Jasmine. Jasmine's had enough loss this year. We're not leaving her colt behind. We're carrying plenty of grain. If there's a problem, it's my problem. Period."

"Fine with me, pardner," Jed said. "Just remember, if that useless horse gets sick and slows you down, you're on your own. The wagon train ain't going to wait for you."

"I've been warned," Jasmine's papa said. "Now, let's finish up our business here and get ready to move on out."

Jed pulled up on his reins real rough-like and went galloping away, and Jasmine's papa went trotting along behind him—treating his horse much nicer.

Leave me behind? Get eaten by wolves? Or coyotes? Not enough grass to eat?

"Don't worry, Koda," Jasmine said, as if

she was reading my mind. "We won't leave you behind. And you won't get eaten by any wild thing. Jed's cross with everyone. Just because he led a wagon train to Oregon last year, he thinks he knows everything about the trail. Papa says he doesn't mean any harm."

Well, I wasn't so sure of that. There was plenty of harm in the way he rode his horse. And even though I didn't know how far two thousand miles was, I knew this: they couldn't leave me behind. I was a quarter horse, the fastest horse alive. I would run after my mama and Jasmine all the way to Oregon, even if I had to tangle with wolves and cougars and coyotes to do it.

Heading Westward to Oregon

The very next morning, before the sun was even up, the wagon train moved out. And we moved with it—Mama and me, Jasmine and her papa, other horses and hundreds of oxen and wagons and humans—a big, long train of us. We headed out, heading west to Oregon.

For many weeks, we moved westward. And I have to say, I didn't like it one little bit. Every day was the same. We got woken up before sunrise by Jed blowing on a bugle. The men rounded up the milk cows and cattle. They hitched up the horses and oxen. Everybody got breakfast, and we moved on out.

And, like I told my mama, I was kept tethered to a wagon like I was just a human child who might wander off and get lost!

I couldn't trot or run or gallop or even crow-hop. The ground was hot and my feet got burned. The dust was so thick, my eyes and nostrils became coated with it. The humans put towels and handkerchiefs over their noses and mouths, and even though Jasmine wiped my face, there were times when I couldn't so much as see the wagon in front of me. All around us was flat country, and alongside, tall grass—so tall that it sometimes came to the tops of the wagons. Hot. Dusty. Windy. Hot. Some days, hail. Then more heat and dust. And the hot wind set the dust to swirling.

Each day, the positions of the wagons got changed so that the front wagons went to the back, and the back wagons went to the front, where it wasn't so dusty. But even on the days when our wagon was near the front, it was almost impossible to see.

Jasmine coughed and coughed. That string of beads she wore around her neck got as brown and dusty as the earth, and so did her clothing. Most humans walked, but some

of the old ones rode in the wagons, and we
went miles and miles every day. Twenty
miles without a single minute to run free and
explore. Yet Mama and the other horses were
all free, galloping on ahead.

I could feel myself becoming sulky and

nervous and out of sorts. If I couldn't run and play, I at least wanted to work, maybe even pull some wagons. Other horses were doing that, and they got to trot right smartly— though I did see how hard that work was. Still, I could do it if they'd let me.

But all Jasmine said to me was, "Koda, I know you're restless. But you're too young to pull a wagon and not strong enough yet for me to ride you. I'm sorry to tether you, but you might run away and get caught by wolves. I can't let anything bad happen to you."

Well, I wouldn't get caught by wolves. I'm a quarter horse. I'm fast. Besides, her little dog, Honey, he ran alongside, and he didn't run away. And so far, he hadn't gotten eaten by wolves.

I wondered how come she didn't understand me anymore.

Each day, when it neared sundown, the men pulled the wagons into circles, sometimes three or four different circles. They hooked the tongue of one wagon into the back of the other one and left a big open space in the middle, like a horseshoe. The humans settled down there and cooked their supper, and the little children frolicked and played inside that circle. After the evening meal, sometimes the men took out guitars and banjos, and men and women danced. Most horses were hobbled outside the circles so that they could graze, unless they were being ridden for guard duty against wolves and outlaws.

But I was kept tethered to a wagon, still!

Most evenings, Mama came to visit with me, and I told her about my hurt feelings. But she had no sympathy for me. *We're all hot and dusty*, is all she ever said. *Be glad you don't have to pull a wagon.*

So that's how it went, days and even weeks going by. And each day, I got more and more sulky. I began to buck and pull against that rope. Jasmine kept walking along with me, sweet-talking me, and sometimes she put Honey up on my back, just to give him a bit of a rest, because his paws were all blistered from the hot sand. I was almost mad enough to buck him off, but I knew he was little and a friend to Jasmine, so I didn't.

Then one day, when Jasmine had turned her head away, I nipped her side a little. She pulled away from me and looked mighty hurt, and I thought she'd sure get mad, maybe even give me a whack on my rump, but she didn't. She just went in the wagon, came back, and gave me a dried-up old apple to chew. She didn't say a word, just gave it to me. I felt bad after that, watching her blinking through that handkerchief she had wrapped around her dusty face, that poor little dog held up in her arms. And when we stopped for the noon hour, she took that handkerchief and dipped it in the water bucket, and she wiped my face. She got all the sand and grit out of my eyes and nose.

"I'm sorry, Koda," she whispered to me. "I know how hard it is on you."

I felt a little ashamed and not angry at her anymore, and I tried to tell her that by rubbing my head up and down against her.

That night, when I saw Mama, it seemed she'd heard about what I'd done, perhaps from the humans, because she said, *Maybe*

Jasmine thinks you're too wild. Could be if you stopped bucking and acting like a wild colt, she'd turn you loose awhile.

Oh, I said. *She would?*

Might, Mama said.

Well. So for the next couple of days, I got real docile. I walked nice and sweet, no bucking, no nothing, just turning my head every little while to look at Jasmine. And I walked real smooth when she put Honey on my back. Then one night, Jasmine called her papa to come and look at me.

"Papa?" she said. "Papa, Koda's acting strange. Do you think he's sick? Does he have colic?"

Her papa looked me over really good, in

my mouth and at my gums, and I wanted to tell him what was wrong.

But he already knew. "Not much wrong that I can see," he said, and he went about scratching me on that nice bumpy place between my ears, and I leaned my head toward him. "I think this here colt needs to run free awhile," he said.

Ah! After that, each night when we stopped, I got to romp around inside the circle of wagons. It wasn't like running on the plains or hills like I'd done with my mama those first days, but it was sure better than being tethered. And then, after a while, when Jasmine saw that I was not so wild and maybe wasn't going to run off, I was let outside the circle for a short time each night. I romped with the older horses while the guards were setting up watch for the night, in case of wolves or Indians who might attack.

One night, after many, many days of flat plains, with nothing but waving grass and scorching sun, we crossed into Nebraska and arrived at a walled fort on the Platte River called Fort Kearny. We stopped there so the wagons could get new supplies. Jasmine's papa had new shoes made for Mama. I heard him tell Jasmine that they cost three dollars each. He also bought medicines and Epsom salts for soaking sore feet.

For so very many more moons, we walked on, westward across the plains, hot and tired and dusty. As we got further west, the land became hilly, rising up and up and up. Some hills were so steep that things slid backward out of the wagons. Once, a tiny girl and her baby brother tumbled from their wagon. Their mama quick grabbed them before they got run over by the wagon wheels. Finally, one night we came to a place called Ash Hollow. There the air was crisp and the water fresh and clean. Breezes blew soft and cool on us, and we rested there a day, our spirits lifted. We were halfway to Oregon. To a place where I could once again run free.

And then one day, a little child became sick. She got sick in the morning and was dead by nighttime. Then more children sickened and died, and grown people, too, old ones and young ones, mamas and papas.

They called it cholera, and it swept over us as fast as a lightning storm. Each day, a new person died, and each night, there was someone new to sorrow over. We stopped to bury the dead, but we didn't stop for long. Jed said that we had to keep going to get over the mountain before the snows fell.

There was so much wailing and crying, it seemed every wagon lost someone. In some wagons, the mama and papa both died, and the little children were left orphans. Then other mamas and papas took them in to care for them. Some of the older boys then helped out by driving the wagon.

Jasmine got pale and tired. And she still coughed.

It wasn't just people who got sick, either.

Horses and oxen sickened and died, too. Mama said it wasn't cholera that killed the animals. Exhaustion and heat did the job just as well, she said. Sometimes the oxen dropped dead right where they stood, still in their harnesses. Even though I wasn't working like other horses or oxen, I became weary, too. My hooves were caked with dirt and sores, and though the wounds closed up at night, they opened again the next day as soon as we started walking that hot earth.

It seemed each day got harder than the last. Even my mama grew weaker. She barely spoke to me, as if she was too weary to talk. It began to seem that Oregon was just a dream. And that things could not get worse.

And then one night, the Indians came.

South Pass

The men were just setting up watch for the night when the alarm bell clanged. "Indians!" they began shouting to one another.

Out against the horizon, horses appeared, and atop the horses, Indians. We had seen Indians at a distance before, and Jasmine had pointed them out to me. But they had never come close. Now they were thundering up to us, the horses snorting and tossing their heads as they were reined in. The Indians had shaved heads, some with little tufts of hair on top. Some of them had painted faces. They stopped in front of us.

I was still outside the circle of wagons, and Jasmine had just come with my lead rope. Now she held herself close to my side and I could feel her tremble.

Behind us, inside the circle of wagons, everyone became still. Even the children didn't cry or speak.

"Oh, Koda!" Jasmine whispered, fingering the beaded string around her neck. "I'm afraid."

I was afraid, too. I had heard stories of how Indians sometimes killed settlers and robbed them of their horses.

Jed was atop his horse, and Jasmine's papa was mounted on my mama. They trotted up beside us. Mama rolled her eyes and snorted and stamped.

One of the Indians said, "Howdy."

Jasmine's papa said "howdy" back.

For a long time, the Indian looked at us. And then he pointed. "Trade!" he said. "That one. Young. Strong." He was pointing—at me!

He held out a buffalo robe.

"Koda?" Jasmine said. "Trade for Koda? No."

"Hush!" Jed said.

"No!" Jasmine said. "I won't hush. No! You can't have Koda."

"Koda," the Indian man said.

Jasmine nodded. "Koda. It's Sioux. It means 'friend.'"

The Indian looked hard at Jasmine. "Your friend?" he asked.

Jasmine nodded. "Yes!" she said.

I *was* her friend! The Indian man wouldn't take me away. From her. From my mama. Would he?

He was quiet for a time. A long time. The only thing I heard was the snorting and stamping of the horses, the switching of tails. Finally the Indian man nodded. "You keep Koda," he said. "Here." And he held out the buffalo robe to her. "A gift."

Jasmine said nothing.

"A gift," the Indian said again.

"Don't trust him," Jed muttered. "He'll put an arrow in your back."

Jasmine left my side. Her papa trotted

beside her. She stepped close to the Indian
man. She reached up and took the buffalo
robe. "Thank you," she said. And then she
unlatched the beaded string from around her
neck. She held it out to him. "A gift," she said.

The Indian nodded. Then he said something quietly to the others. The tribe whirled their horses around and disappeared into the night.

After that, some folks said that Jasmine and the Indians had brought us good luck. Because Indians never approached us again. And the cholera seemed to fade away as fast as it had come. Jasmine didn't sicken with cholera, but she kept coughing and coughing, and I could see that she was growing mighty weary, too. She also looked different, thin and lean and as brown as the earth. She worked hard at keeping up my spirits, however, even though I knew she was feeling mighty low herself.

"Home," she whispered to me each morning. "Not much further, Koda. A mountain home. You can run free. Soon. I promise. You can run and play and even crow-hop again!"

And then one morning, just after we had started out, a huge cry went up from the men on horseback up ahead. The Cascades! The mountains! We could see the mountains. Once we were up and over the mountains, we'd be home. Home in Oregon.

And I'd be free!

Well, it seemed everyone's spirits were as high as the mountains when we stopped for the noon meal, though Jed warned that the hardest part was ahead, taking those wagons and oxen over the mountains. Still, folks felt easier, and later, when we stopped for the night, they even brought out the guitars and banjos, and there was music for the first time in a long while. I looked for Jasmine, knowing how happy she would be. I wanted her to rub that spot between my ears and tell me again, "Home, Koda. You'll be home and free." But I didn't see her anywhere, so I figured she was off dancing with the guitar-playing folks. Though I remembered then that she hadn't walked with me since the noon meal. And when we stopped for the night, it was her uncle Henry who had loosed me from my tether.

Even the horses were friskier that night, heads up, sniffing that mountain air. I was running free with them, but after a while, I didn't feel so free and happy. Something was worrying me. Wolves? Coyotes? I turned my head up and sniffed the air. No.

Indians? No, the Indians had been friendly, hadn't bothered us at all. Was it bears? Folks had talked of bears, but we'd not seen any. Still, something was wrong. Jasmine? I needed her. Where was she? I lifted my head and whinnied for her.

Nothing. I whinnied again. And again.

No answer.

Mama heard, though, and came trotting up to me.

Mama? I said. *Jasmine. Something's wrong.*

The sickness? Mama asked.

No, I said. *She's gone.*

Mama tossed her head and rolled her

eyes, nervous-like. And just as we were worrying, Jasmine's papa and Jed came hurrying
up, Jasmine's papa on foot, Jed atop his horse.
I could tell that they were worrying, too.

"Koda!" her papa said. "Where's Jasmine?
I was hoping she was with you. Or with
Rosie! Have you seen her? Nobody's seen her
for hours. We've looked and looked."

Of course he didn't expect us to answer,
but he knew that we would if we could.

"We'll keep on looking," Jed said. "But I
got to tell you, Mark, if she's not found by
morning, we're moving on out. We can't
wait for no one. There's already snow in the
mountains."

Jasmine's papa didn't answer, just ran

ahead to some wagons while Jed wheeled his horse around and away from us.

And then I saw something that scared me more than anything had scared me in my whole entire life—even more than that foul-smelling cougar. What I saw was a bunch of those buzzards Mama had told me about way back when I'd just been born. *They're mean old birds. Come only when something is dead or dying,* she'd said. Now a crowd of them was circling high, high in the sky, far away, back the way we had come, high above the grassy hillside, circling around and around.

Mama! I said. *Mama! Buzzards!*

My mama pawed the ground for a bit. *Might not be Jasmine,* she said at last. *Lots of dead and dying things in this desert. Could be an ox or two.*

But it might be Jasmine, I said. *And Mama, she'll die of thirst. I haven't seen her since the noon meal.*

All around us then, folks were hurrying from wagon to wagon, calling her name. More men on horseback came thundering by.

Mama? I said again.

She didn't answer.

My mind was racing: *Buzzards. Move on out? Leave Jasmine behind?*

I knew Mama was thinking those things, too.

I can find her, Mama, I said. *I have a good nose. I can find my way back here, too. My eyes are good and strong. All I have to do is head toward the mountains. I'm strong, Mama.*

Still, my mama hesitated. I knew what she was thinking. That I could get lost, too. That I could get eaten up by wolves. Or coyotes or cougars or even bears.

I'm fast, Mama, I said. *I'm a quarter horse. I'm fast. And young.*

Yes, Mama said, *you are. Go! Go find her.*

I'll come back, I said. *I will.* I turned my head once more up to the sky and looked where those buzzards were circling.

Run! my mama said. *Run hard, my little one.*

Rescue

I gathered my legs under me and lit out back the way we'd come, running like I hadn't run since we'd left on this journey. All that stored-up energy just flowed into my legs, and I took in huge gulps of air. I kept looking toward the sky, to the place where the buzzards circled, but I didn't slow or break stride.

Rocks and pebbles slid beneath my hooves as I surged forward, but I never lost my footing. I could feel my heart thundering in my chest, bringing blood to my legs, my bones, carrying me along.

Faster and faster I ran. Further and further I went, sand and dust almost choking me. The sky was darkening, but I could still see those buzzards circling.

And then, suddenly, the buzzards disappeared, and only one still circled. Where were the others? Had they settled their horrid bodies and beaks and talons already onto the ground—onto Jasmine?

No! I saw them again—two, then three

of them, lifting their heavy bodies back into the sky. Was she alive? Had she been able to chase them away? Was it even Jasmine out there—or some other dying critter? And if it wasn't Jasmine, where was she?

I ran harder, feeling my sides heaving, my breath coming in gasps. But there was young strength in me, and my hooves pounded the dirt. On and on I flew. And then I looked up and the buzzards were almost directly overhead, but not above the path. They circled over the high grass. Waiting. Their caws and cries echoed over the empty land as I abandoned the path and thundered off into the tall grass.

I slowed. Nothing. No Jasmine. Nothing stirring. Just the buzzards overhead.

And then I saw something—two somethings. A buzzard. It crouched on the ground, its ugly bare head bent forward, its eyes glittering at me. And a short way from the buzzard, a small heap lay on the ground.

I roared up to the buzzard, rearing up on my hind legs, boxing furiously with my front hooves. The creature just hopped backward, out of my reach, flapping its nasty wings.

I turned then to the heap on the ground. Jasmine. And beside her, her dog, Honey. Neither of them moved. Their eyes were shut.

Wake up, wake up, I shouted inside me. I drummed my hooves hard on the ground, close to Jasmine's head, so hard that the ground trembled.

Don't be dead, don't be dead! I told her. I

nudged her head hard with mine. *Get up, get up!*

I nudged her harder. Her mouth and lips were cracked and swollen. But her eyelids fluttered. *Get up, get up!*

She opened her eyes a moment and then closed them again. I nudged her even harder. Harder. This was no time to be gentle. And then her eyes opened again, really opened, and I knew that she had seen me. She reached for Honey and dragged his limp body close to her.

"Koda?" she whispered.

Up, I told her. *Up. On my back. Hurry. It will be dark soon.*

Could I make her understand? How could I get her up on my back? *Stand up,* I told her. *Stand.* I was ordering her inside my head. Did she understand? She must!

Up! I told her again. *Stand.* I drummed my hooves against the ground.

She gathered herself to her feet, swaying. She wrapped Honey in her petticoat. I inched closer to her. If she could just grasp my mane.

She did. She pulled herself toward me. She tried to climb up. But she slid off sideways. "Koda!" she whispered. "Can't. Water. Can't."

Well, she could. I wouldn't leave her here. But I pretended to. I meandered away, the way my mama did when I was just a colt, and I'd had to follow.

"Koda!" she whispered.

I came back. I came close. I tried to fold my front legs the way I did when I was about to crow-hop. I attempted to get close to the ground, close.

Jasmine tried again, holding tight to my mane. And then she was on my back— wobbly and off center, but she was up there. I could feel her. And I could feel that she was holding tight to Honey, too. I had never taken anyone on my back, and she felt strange, her body hot against mine, hot the way noon sun felt against my back. She wasn't heavy, though, and I knew I could take her weight.

I turned back to the path. I had to light out toward the mountains before it was dark, before the wolves and coyotes came out. Before Jasmine died of thirst. I had to be careful, too—be smooth. If Jasmine fell off again, she might not have the strength to climb back up.

I broke into a smooth trot, then a gallop, fast but steady . . . steady. . . .

And so on into the night we went, Jasmine clinging to my mane, her head now slumped against my neck. On toward the mountain, toward camp, and toward home.

Late October, 1848

And now we are home.

We climbed into the Cascades, and nights became cold, but even after all the heat, folks did not rejoice much. They were just too tired. Fights even broke out as men had to take apart the wagons to haul them over the mountain, then put them together again. Some wagons got away coming down the mountain, tumbled and split into pieces. Two oxen drowned while crossing the river.

But finally they did it. We all did it. We are now in the valley. It's fertile and green, just the way Jasmine said it would be. The humans are picking out plots of land and marking them off. Jasmine's papa chose land with a rolling hillside that he says is perfect for horses.

"Just for Koda," he says. And he rubs that spot between my ears and talks to me, and sometimes, I think he even weeps. But I know they are happy tears. He says he's getting a new herd of horses to help him clear

the land, and I'll have company. And he says that I can run and gallop and play.

He's building the most perfect house for him and Jasmine, he says, and he tells me thank you, thank you, thank you, over and over again.

I told Mama that he was so grateful he might even build me my very own house if I wanted.

Mama says I shouldn't get a big head.

When I had galloped back into camp that night, Jasmine had tumbled from my back into her papa's arms, and someone had lifted the little dog, too. Folks had poured water over Jasmine and Honey. They gave them both ladles full of water to drink, and of course I got water, too, buckets and buckets of water to drink, and rubdowns and blankets. And after a while, Jasmine sat herself up and talked to us and cradled that little dog in her arms. And there was such rejoicing.

She said how Honey had wandered away during the noon meal and she'd gone after him. She found him just a little ways away, in the high grass, happily resting his feet, which were so sore from the hot sand. And so she rested, too, in that grassy spot. And fell asleep. When she woke and looked around, the wagons were all gone. She stood up, the grass waving all about her, and could see nothing. Not even dust.

And then later—much later—when she was sure that she would die of thirst and heat—I had come for her.

Jasmine and her papa, and even Jed, make me out to be a hero. I don't feel like a hero, but maybe I don't know what heroes feel like. But my mama is very proud of me, too, I can tell.

Now I've become accustomed to wearing a saddle, and in the early mornings, Jasmine comes out and saddles me up, and her papa comes and saddles Mama, and we ride together. We ride all over this huge green place, and at night, when the stars come out, I'm free to roam and run, just as Jasmine promised I could.

Sometimes I go flying all over, racing the wind, and other times, I just stop and think. I look up at the stars, at the trees waving their branches in the moonlight, and I think:

I'm here, and it's beautiful, just as Jasmine said it would be. I'm young, and I've learned so much, and there's so much more to learn and see. And I think, too, of all that I've done. We've done. Jasmine promised, and she was right. We made it. We're home.

APPENDIX

MORE ABOUT
THE QUARTER HORSE

History

The first horses in America were of mostly
Spanish descent, brought here by Columbus
on his second journey in 1493. Later, in the

1600s, other colonists arrived, bringing horses from Ireland and England. When these breeds were mixed, the amazing quarter horse developed. The resulting horses were well muscled and strong, and the characteristic they were best known for, besides their strength and sweet nature, was speed.

Colonists enjoyed horse racing, and at the end of a long day's work on the farm or ranch, men took their horses into town for races. Betting on horses was common in those days, and it was said that many fortunes were won and lost on those races. It is likely that even children raced their horses, though if there were bets, they were not for money. Rather, prestige and bragging rights were what was on the line.

The simple race usually took place along the only available flat, well-traveled span—the main street. Since in the 1600s most main streets were a quarter mile long, the horses that excelled came to be called quarter milers, or eventually, quarter horses. The first recorded quarter horse race is believed to have taken place in Henrico County, Virginia, in 1674.

Outside of the races, the quarter horse was most useful when it came to doing heavy chores, such as farmwork that involved pulling wagons and plows and clearing trees and rocks from the land. This horse also earned a reputation as a spectacular "cow horse." It had a unique ability to head off a cow or calf that needed to be roped or singled out. As the 1800s came along, ranchers drove

their herds many miles cross-country to market, and the quarter horse kept the animals from escaping, easily moving a drifting cow back into the herd.

The country continued to expand west in the 1800s, and the pioneers moved their horses with them. Sometimes these horses were used to pull wagons along the Oregon Trail because horses could cover distance far more rapidly than oxen. Most ox-drawn wagons could go at best twenty miles a day, whereas the horse-pulled wagons might move twice that distance. However, good feed is essential for a healthy horse, and grass along the trail was spotty at best. To offset that, some settlers carried their own grain for the horses, but this added dramatically to the weight of the wagon, and therefore meant more stress on the horses. It also cost a lot more, so only the wealthiest travelers were able to afford it. Also, many horses sickened and died on the trail, despite the best care that could be given, and so oxen became the preferred animal for this undertaking.

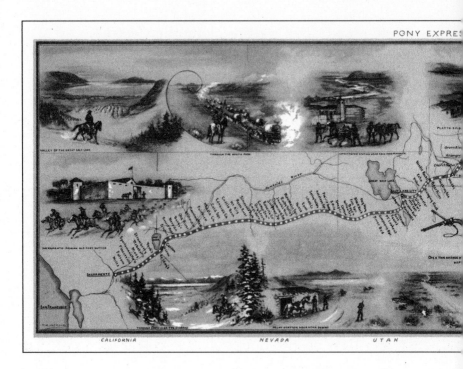

In 1860, the Pony Express began. Quarter horses were a good choice for this endeavor also. Whereas the oxen and wagon would take almost six months to complete the journey

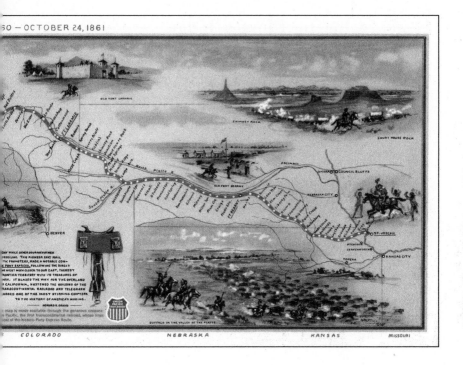

from Missouri to Oregon, the quarter horse
on the Pony Express made that journey in
just eight days! (Of course, he had no weight
but the saddlebags and the rider.)

Quarter Horses Today

Today, there are many events besides simple racing in which quarter horses continue to compete—barrel racing, cow roping, and team penning, among others.

Quarter horses were not recognized as a breed until 1940. Before that, they were considered rather like dogs without a pedigree—the mutts of the horse world. But like many mutts, the quarter horse was a wonderfully mannered and pleasant creature. In fact, today, its gentle disposition is one of its characteristic features.

So how do you know if the horse you are looking at is a quarter horse? Besides its great speed and gentle demeanor, you will note heavy muscling and powerful, rounded hindquarters. Its head is small and its eyes are wide and pleasant. Some say that one can see kindness in a quarter horse's eyes. At one time, only solid-color horses were recognized as true quarter horses, but that has changed, and the registry allows certain other markings. There are now over three million quarter horses in the world, and they are universally known and loved by their owners—as the best horses in the world!

⤳ COMING IN APRIL 2010! ⤳

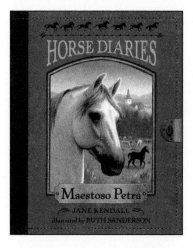

Vienna, Austria, 1938

Maestoso Petra is a world-famous Lipizzaner stallion. He has spent years in the Spanish Riding School, training to perform the complex airs above the ground that only Lipizzaners can accomplish. But when World War II breaks out in Europe, he learns to think less about performing and more about survival. Here is Maestoso Petra's story . . . in his own words.

About the Author

Patricia Hermes is the author of over forty novels for children and young adults and two nonfiction books for adults.

As a child, she fell in love with horses and spent many a day (and night) "stealing" rides bareback on a neighbor horse who grazed in a nearby field. However, since she grew up in and around New York City, and since horseback riding was an expensive proposition, there weren't many opportunities for lessons. Later, though, when she got older and moved, there was much more opportunity to connect with her beloved horses, especially in places like Virginia and

Connecticut. She no longer had to "steal" rides, but began taking riding lessons, and was particularly attracted to—and challenged by—a classically beautiful type of riding called dressage, also sometimes called horse ballet. Although she has never "owned" a horse, many horses have owned her heart.

A resident of Connecticut, and the mother of five, she frequently speaks at schools and conferences around the country.

About the Illustrator

Ruth Sanderson grew up with a love for horses. She drew them constantly, and her first oil painting, at age fourteen, was a horse portrait.

Ruth has illustrated and retold many fairy tales and likes to feature horses in them whenever possible. Her book about a magical horse, *The Golden Mare, the Firebird, and the Magic Ring*, won the Texas Bluebonnet Award in 2003. She illustrated the first Black Stallion paperback covers and a number of chapter books about horses, most recently *Summer Pony* and *Winter Pony* by Jean Slaughter Doty.

Ruth and her daughter have two horses, an Appaloosa named Thor and a quarter horse named Gabriel. She lives with her family in Massachusetts.

To find out more about her adventures with horses and the research she did to create the illustrations in this book, visit her Web site, www.ruthsanderson.com.

⪜ Collect all the books in the ⪜
Horse Diaries series!

Elska

CATHERINE HAPKA
illustrated by RUTH SANDERSON

Bell's Star

ALISON HART
illustrated by RUTH SANDERSON

⪜ And coming soon ⪜

Koda

PATRICIA HERMES
illustrated by RUTH SANDERSON

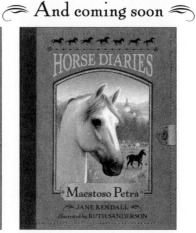

Maestoso Petra

JANE KENDALL
illustrated by RUTH SANDERSON